song trials

song trials

Mxolisi Nyezwa

POETRY
Gecko

Published by Gecko Poetry
an imprint of University of Natal Press
Private Bag X01, Scottsville 3209
South Africa

ISBN: 0 86980 976 8

Publication of this poetry collection has been facilitated by grants from the Roy Joseph Cotton Poetry Trust, the Arts and Culture Trust of the President, Buchu Books and the National Arts Council.

ARTS &
CULTURE
TRUST

NATIONAL **ARTS** COUNCIL
OF SOUTH AFRICA

Edited by Robert Berold, ISEA, Rhodes University
Cover graphic: "Elalini" Series No. 1 by Mxolisi Sapeta (oil on canvas)
Photograph of author by Ewald Kruger
Cover design by Welma Odendaal
Layout by Lesley Lewis, Inkspots, Durban
Printed by Interpak Books, Pietermaritzburg

Versions of these poems have appeared in:

Botsotso, Cape Times, Carapace, Essential Things, Grocott's Mail,
Incanda, Kotaz, Kunapipi, Lava of this Land, New Coin,
New Contrast, New Nation, Poetry of the 90s, Sesame,
Sounds of Silence, Staffrider, Sunbelly Press, Tribute, Upstream
and Writing from Here.

To Tate, for not ceasing to dream with us

Contents

IV

V

I

I cannot think of all the pains

i cannot think of all the pains in men's breasts
without the urge to sleep, or to lie down, i cannot think
without seeing God's face in the child's smile,
or in the lonely cry in the night and in the sea.

i cannot think of all the pains that have come
and gone, pains in men's waists
and in men's shoes –
i cannot have relief proper, wearing a neat tie.

i run around in circles, like sprinkling water,
i can't have true relief, swearing out loud
and counting out the pains in my breast,
and in my pants.

i cannot think of all the pains and all the years wasted,
all the craze of lonely men in village rooms,
and all the bodies that lie out cold, in avoided streets –
i can't run out old, like a joyful child

and watch a sky pregnant with pain, or with turbulent rain;
i cannot think of the soil without lying down,
i cannot think of tears, lonely geographies
and the third world, without the urge to cry or to sit down.

things change

for Malope

at least then, it won't be like this
it will be a totally new suffering
like when a baby sucks his thumb.

it will be a totally new experience
(for God and history has provided)
we won't have to blow our minds
about it.

it will be like a fresh song
from a sparkling songbird
it will be like that for us, as an old
woman sits neglected
on the chair of her memories
it will be fresher, more vital
for us ... at least it won't be like death.

and like the death we die
every moment of our lives
it will be a totally new suffering
it will be like a song sung free
from a careless heart ...

(our failure will have its dignity.)

it all begins

it all begins with thunder in the middle of the road,
it begins with people bleeding from the intestine –
it begins with one statement,
with the scratch of one pen.
it begins with the smell of death dying
with people of all sizes in every epoch
shouting from the grave.

it begins with the man in the personnel department,
it begins with the smell of frying eggs
the brief passage and elongation/reflux of time,
on the contrary –
it begins with the promise of peace
in the avalanche of lies.

and it could be all these things
as it yawns in the morning
with the blunder bearing on us
with the emergence of summer
the fire of history closes its doors behind us
and sunk geniuses walk about
aimlessly through the air –

and it all begins
and it will never cease.

dementia

i have two organs working against me,
i have two thoughts, two words
eagerly – that break my heart.

i have two bottles of brandy, an ale of rum
fresh flour and an ounce of salt –
i have two terrible thoughts breathing down my spine.

in my finger and in my broken tail
i have two snails that stop my blood spurt,
that drive me madly wild.

at break point

i am drinking winter from a cup,
paper worms agitating the uMnga tree.
set gates, on which kids swing
deathly musical in the wind.

huge texts, bristled intellect and warped
varsity thesis,
i grope through the history of my ignorance
pleased to break free.

in the shadow, beneath the apple tree
men dig for diamonds and for gold.
backwards i lift
the imagined horrors of my anatomical jail.

walking

i keep still. in my shirt and in my element
i feel the vein's tremor, the heart's pulse,
the weed through the skull, through a piece of air
around my skull.

i see the unstable dark sea, furious
and on my back, my spine, the vertebral sky.
i look the cold stranger in the eye,
the looming humour, earth's forgotten smiles.

i walk the length in an unbending street.
i knock down a bird's wing. i see a universe
speeding down a broken sky. i don't stop.
i see men circling towards an unmoving crowd.

diviner's bones

recently i wrote a letter
like i knew how,
of riverbanks, of milestones
premonitions of another world.

i thought i saw you in a dream,
we, together beside a hearse.
a man comes through as i sleep,
still clutching a spear like a god.

i was bored after all that talk
and all that walk in avenues with no light,
lamp-lights long blurred
like smear in one's eyes.

song trials

I

what can i say
which i never said
and never dreamt or betrayed slowly,
till they rattle the old bones down in the sea,
till the pack of thieves return home with the breath
of their dead singing
and their heavy chains, till i welt in my skin like a wound
tired down in waiting.

and i feel the full terror of sunlight in my eyes
i feel the implacable destiny of pain
lying like sand-roses on a floor,

i can't bear it no more!
even in singing, and in talking aloud
no sound comes out, no horse flies out
through the door like sun-rays through snow.

and how much can you weigh my land
bullets and dreams that fall
assassinated every day,
i was alone fighting there, alone
in a war without drums, in a fierce battle
when terror broke out from the sky.

and their lessons they learnt with bowed down whispers
in their songs, with simple praises
that doubled each minute in excruciating pain –
and they left me alone there,
with robust horrors in my mind.

II

it is the plain mustard oil that is killing me,
and there's a death that is sent over to me like the sky
by five kind men over the sea with the north wind.

the dead lady claws her way to sleep
to mummify the soul
and the poison of distress is slowly tearing off the snake's eyes.

i never heard the night shudder,
i never stood on the balcony on the wooden bridge
to greet sunrise
to betray the rose
and the little things i possess now that are my life's blood
are the little wounds of my soul.

i had gathered the pale blossom in my eye
in order to see the snow,
in the fields of green moss
i could hear the voice the blood spilt in silence
on the white snow.

in the house with three cellars there are drunkards with sick minds
and the camel's back drags the horse of blue crimes
towards the stream
towards the hobble of mute souls.

in the house there are knives with nine lives
in the house of the big dog (where there were no shadows)
there are shadows with thick skins.
and the empty greed of sick children
splits open the kegs and the throats of men.

III
i proclaim to the sky THUNDER!
i proclaim to the mystic flag of robberies a strife without
                                    contemplation!
i declare a disease to the sea-shores, i declare disease to the
                                    sea-horse
lung cancer to the octopus, then i am happy!
for i won't know the flight of the dragonfly
i won't feel the hunger that seeps through the night
inside the veins of the anemone,
inside the cough of the seventh heaven.

i declare to the false man his falsity
and give to the sea-brothel its prostitutes!

i declare to the voice that is dead more seaweed a thousand times!
i declare to the deadman his own brandy — NAKEDNESS!
and the bones of boipatong live in front of us
inside the wine's goblet, beneath the hooves of the old mule.

i don't believe in the curse inside the tasteless white powder:
i want to be the reed and the canoe and the motionless aloe,
i want to be the tiny posture, the mysterious wind driving a
                                    witch-hunt,
to smell the juice inside a drunken murder —

upstairs, in the house of men in black robes and white wigs
a murder is contemplated,
in the house of the King and the lecherous Queen of England
your teeth are showing off their cruel fangs!

the children are gone

no longer strange
no longer.
like the earth
like the human spirit
it's not strange,
not unfamiliar –
we have left those feelings
many rains ago.

they are dead within us,
transformed
into the human void
that re-chains our empty clarity,
that sculpts each man's fate,
and breast-feeds our poverty –
we have left them,
abandoned.

it is not new
we tell them – that is
should they ask
have the strength to inquire
"where's Thokozile, where's Dumizulu?"
and we look at them
with only cold tears in our eyes.

obligatory visits

when they told me the news
i remembered there's so much to do.
the letters to be posted,
the obligatory visits to be made.

i recalled how quietly the child sleeps at night,
the eyes like silk curtains drawn, retreat from light –
i once sat in a street in New Brighton
and watched the mulberry leaves sway in the wind.

i made unending melodies to myself,
recalled how time draws the heart to its end,
thought of things that vanish all the while,
in front of our eyes, in no time.

the poet's failure

we had words in us that we never said.
we could stand in these waterless alleys
and march into the wet rain.

we smelled like starved rogues, we stank
like dying corpses
sailing the warm winds of our silence,
searching in reckless shelters to cool our lips.

we struggled begging conciliation
down the trodden tracks of cold hurricanes.
seeking out lost igloos,
we had words within these day-long blues –

driven by cold emotions into the shades and shadows
of a dying land, we had words that choked to be said –
and we never said them.

minute

my anxiety is all over
like a bloodied town
where they locked the beggars away
and a travelling troupe of dancers
and circus clowns
leaves the alarm clocks
chiming out of tune
against the walls.

and it is with strained effort
that no more will the Sunday jamboree of death
fill up the death halls
it is with a sad longing
for my sequestered being
that i count out my living days
one after the other
in my fury's last blaze.

the man gone

for Seko

a man is defined by ladders,
by walks upstairs, or downstairs,
by skills acquired returning home
or escaping the rain.

the man known yesterday is not the man you meet,
forever, around the corner, in Brussels
or in the street, in York Road in Umtata
selling newspapers and coke.

that man is lost forever, like a packet of chips.
his feet supine and delirious when he sleeps –
like a felled bush in the forest
he is never known.

I may laugh for the sound

i may laugh for the sound
of sunshine against my palate,
the peasant who damns the street,
who demands all weather.

i may laugh for the memory that holds
together your pain, for them the doctors
who cut open all wounds.

and they that see their christenings on wings
that fan, they that flow in regiments in streets
on day-to-day turns,
they, your brothers, your betrayers – men.

charity

i can say it's been twenty odd years
teaching myself to give to charity properly,
with no head for figures,
a few rands in my pocket.

i think it started by dying at night,
being bullied at school, enjoying sex,
my treatise on Marx
and being a father of ten.

now i mistletoe out at the eavesdrop
of friends.

you will sing me a song

you will sing me a song,
i will sit still, and listen –
and at the hour of despair
i will jostle and participate in your dance
the amazing dance to your melody.

before the years passed
men thought rhythm stays simple and true,
that regarding mankind
he came from the Far East, that from there
men wore charms
and men hungered for extinction and disfigurement.

but who today remains still in your cool tunes
that you whisper out like the wind, in Alexandria
in KwaNongoma, in Crossroads, in Afrika –
who cuddles the steady flame

who sits and straddles the sullen inextinguishable earth
as the riddle and the dance deceive
the house built by wholesome men.

once in time you're robbed all over

for Vusumzi

once in time you're robbed all over,
and your body has its time.
you move all over, and you're ash
and cold inside.

under the room where your selves are
he wobbles your body like a slate
from side to side.

by all means you move all your doors,
the lamp-posts, the folded knees in,
you remove yourself from his language –

the mouth he speaks, the language
his words kick.

just for us the lips

just for us the lips
which nobody dares to move.
the furious rings of earth God places
in someone's hand.

for us these tears, the streams that flower and bloom
crushing petals on our bare hands, for us
the slayings, the dead, the waiting
that shall rise up again.

meeting mr jesus

they say that on the last day men will burn forever.
transvestites will walk free; conversations will stop –
and love-sick mermaids will be taken from the seas.
they say some men will carry spades all around –
and all around New Brighton beach, shipwrecks
absent-mindedly will lurch; and the water-bugs
and the spiders will creep through the empty dorps.

I believe

i believe man is born free,
i believe man is born spiritual and clean –
presentiments, conflicts with family and cigarette smokes
intensify man's vision of suicide.

i believe the man in Siberia somehow relates
and is related to the man in Rwanda, in Afrika,
and both men sometimes will pick up the hoe and in the soil
plant: beans, onions, oranges and the cocoa tree.

i believe therefore that man is born good and clean,
we only make him otherwise for one reason or another.

song of beauty

for Sindiswa

now listen to me, no almonds grow in spring
and there is no moon, no one star
nor baby cry disturbs the silence.

everyday we sing of dying
everyday the sea will wash our blood to claim us
and no one will know.

but if you have to know
last night i didn't sleep, i dreamt of dying.
i went out in the night and planted seedlings
and the night was diseased,
all pitiful and dreadful ailments yelled at me.

but for me is enough to say i'm no longer dead, but live.
it suffices to say the universe also sprouts its tentacles of blood,
and there's a rich flower from my shoulder to my hand,
in what was beautiful, in what was growing impossibly thin.

for now i'm no longer dead but live in the soil's core
the mist of the land covers my sins –

now listen to me, for there's no one outside.

III

a direction is never lost

for Khuselo

a direction is never lost
like a man moving east to west
huddled in thin light, a hermit's hut –
well-battered spoors lead like arterioles
into a man's home – his heart.

love poem

your lips are full of thunder.
in my mind your eyes open,
are full of gold –
are numb.

some fanfare resides there,
stars fall, are splattered
on tiny shoots, on seeds
beneath the grass, in the windmill's shade.

quiet place

and it seems that i live in a quiet place
at the end of time
with a blowing universe behind me.

i remain aware of the long-suffering of things
i remain aware with a simple truth
of how the planet eventually crumbles.

to me there is always the spaza shop at the end of the street,
the vague colour of the moon
and of the southern sky.

good woman

i love you like a peasant
in humble places
and after the September rain has breathed its stinkwood tree
in all the right places, i'll be like a poplar tree
hanging from the virgin wall.

happiness

for Saphokazi

i know i have forgotten you
like the sea that forgets the blue sky, like the sun
that forgets to heat the land,
a pain so deep settles in all familiar places,
and i am deeply disturbed, and i am sad.

i wrestle with the quills of madness:
dead melodies of joy, where will i find you?
i know i have missed you with a number so deep,
and what the eye doesn't see, my heart feels.

a sea-shell sings to me the music of earth,
the last soil sells to me a heritage,
the madness of the land heals my name.

some think of the universe

some think of the universe as a street,
with a kilometre, perhaps a mile
that informs of unidimensions.
and maybe, they say, the universe is broad
too broad, like a pavement, or a bridge,
people fill up its dimensions.

i think of the universe rather dimly,
in gloomy terms, as one god who never sleeps,
who stretches the whole length
who never jorls or parties,
who certainly never mourns humanity's follies.

and like ants on a petal
people forever on his face will move,
and never stop.

geographical land

at each place i meet my silent river,
and on the geographical land
in the stars of my country
flash my green colour of rose.

in the spy in the eye of the tiger
there's a common descent that looks like murder.
in the iced thigh of my wife
a green devout man who holds the colour purple.

i have free-fallen
        (my eternal friends in the streets of my dirty town will say)
buried my head underneath the sand.
i have seen the earth purple, the leaves holding their grass,
the strangest things (heavens from the roots of heavens!) tripping
and fall.

i have looked disaster in the eye until one spade from the loot
of heaven fell down below and cried,
the great oceans surprised me with their thinking,
the great broken sigh of the fire-fly.

eight voices of sorrow

1

today i'm surrounded by an aura of green leaves
like the sky is surrounded by water,
when the yellow moth builds its small coccon
near the well
i will dwell in my garden like a butterfly
without my wings.

2

until what surrounds me is not the voice of pity
until what i suffer as my happiness grieves in the synagogues
holding a green flag
the mist will linger in my eye like the moisture of death
or hashish in the air.

3

in the world the beautiful sky collects its impatient rage
and every movement in every sky
is neither felt below its surface
nor inside the woman's tears.

4

in the world which is black with suffering
in the world which has forgotten how to smile
in the world which has forgotten the trickle of death
i walk my dog like a weary man.

5

today in the streets of Zwide
i make it clear to the words of my pain
and i breathe the bitch of the whore
today i kiss the sand of my body
after a time too long
the rain plunges its hands inside my body.

6

everyday you are here like the night
and you disappear at the light of day,
your sanity is accustomed to my jail
your smile has subdued its shadow in the hazel flower
and your gentle stroke is the harsh strike of heaven.

7

today i'm surrounded by an immense suffering
by its tribulation which is my place of crucifix
and sorrow grows against the gentle strike of midnight
and the wave collapses in the depths of the sea
and the moisture of creeping fungus
plunges my head in its arms.

8

and today the flower of my madness is undeterred
today the skeletons of Malaisha grow downwards
towards his grave
and the beautiful voice of my people is felt
like coarse blood on a beautiful day.

day

as an ordinary man,
as a man persecuted i'm easy to know –
and in the green cupboard
where morning stars from a wandering sky
come to meet, would hear my chaos,
and i wouldn't understand
why my speech, the sound of my teeth munching
the dance of the green elves
always rose an hour before dawn.
and in the day i would wait for my day
dressed in long robes.

growing old

and in the years of my decline
i'll stay put in bed, for the fear of water,
for death is written on candle-water,
on the church-stone, before the picking of corn
and men were evolved from the sea,
before all that – iGqili was simply a stream.
i'll stay put in bed and not move
except to say my prayers, or to sleep still.
and in the daylight i'll fumble across the road
and listen to cars roaring by.

like nothing exists anymore

i will live like nothing exists anymore
and in the saddest month
at the strike of 4, i will go out in the rain
praying alas nothing at all will happen.

the old horse which doesn't whine is no longer mine,
he belongs to the other,
in this house the twangs of death breeze through
without an end.

i have ridden the lame horse in snow,
catastrophes play the sweetest note
with a shocking signal,
like glints from fire-flies.

simple poems

today i walked on top of a hill like Moses,
and i felt alone, like someone locked alone in prison.

today i had no idea of time, of human hands
and i could not breathe. nothing at all was happening.

today i committed myself wholeheartedly to the finest things
in life, to write the simple poems

and to sing line by line
the cry of geese.

from the barracks

my mother says:
too much of anything brings emptiness
too much thought
clogs the mind
too much fury
fails the heart.

so too much of anything is an inner emptiness:
too much love
pains the heart
too much sadness
wearies the bones.

and inside the vacuums of our lives
the universe is a turntable
spinning endlessly.

reconciliation

you are more half-dead
than i could ever be.
more deliberate
more dead
and your theory is a valediction of lies
a denial of half-truths
and angry eyes.

you are more of a muse
a magician
with a careful wand.
you are the mother spider
half-deliberate
and fussy.

i sit here with resounding energy
with passive retardation
and if ever the wind should start
if ever Leonardo
should feel my lust –
now.

the whole world is lying
on the Sabbath
of this hour
a summer day drifts by
from all the houses
we see children go
with mouths and eyes wide open
flies of memory
the blue fists of God.

and he is my enemy
the man
who draws into his house
the fluids of Jews
out of human consideration
out of desire or tiredness
the ludicrous Bible
of deformed notions
of plants
of insects
of men who rush the shrieks
of compassion
the solemn sea
over the solemn sea.

come
with your busts of air
your sculptures of gifts

come with your mental rose
down to the wonderful hole
of human error

nothingness
if it troubles you, must trouble you

oppression
if it's a new theme will be shut before your eyes

come
with your busts of air
your sculptures of gifts

this chair that you're sitting on is empty
please –
i'm still your brother-man.

forgive me for the single spot of truth
forgive me for the unique quiver
the exalted spasm.

this chair, this chair
haunts me

and if i'm not free
who's to say more
if i'm not sensible, if i'm not found there?

and if i'm not
if i'm not at the ankles, at the bells of time
if i'm not there to see my face beneath the belly-button
of time, if i'm not
not myself
as the wrinkles of my face and beneath the toes
gather, please
i'm your brother.

the world must moan a long time
and when you return
the pyramids
and the ruins will laugh at you.

for you're still my brother
with your seedy curses pronounced
with your green sentence read.

and your mountain-high
your east love, your vorster square
your thrown-away
your skirmish misses, your blunders.

i'm still, still –

with anxiety, with the simple crab
the fastidious silence
the disconcerting calm.

and you hide me, away from everything
all the things you have known
the overwhelmed places of blood
all the mutilations.

and you're still my friend, nowhere
where i hurt you
and you hurt me.

IV

last poem

ultimately i've been away, on sabbatical
in the cold month of June, without a jersey.
my only girlfriend was a humble girl from Motherwell,
a weary township in PE
where logic has been doomed.

and these excursions of my mind
would have been without exception
repeated in an entire month
with wriggling grotesque worms
tearing the flesh away.

sea

the sea is so heavy inside us
and i won't sleep tonight.
i have buckets of memory in a jar
that i keep for days and nights like these.

gathering

i had gathered the fruits of the universe in my hands
in order to see the bright sky. nothing.
in the sky
not a single child.

in the fields of thorns my brothers build the road.
in the fields of dark betrayal
i had gathered the mist of the rose.

below what appeared remorseful was without sleep,
below the valley of the old lady,
a black sky that was daunting.

i had gathered the truth of my words in a cup
and i could not hear the plea for mercy again.

stray child

a hundred miles from home,
weak-hearted, and thinking of ghosts –
you winter out in farmland shelters
like a frosted wild-bird.

to feel you're free who knows,
you move through burnt land cautious as the wind;
and you're gagged again in your mother's lap,
licking the breast and the puzzles of history.

i have forgotten your form. i collide with doors
without reason or shame.
i walk thick-drugged and dumb.
i describe a world simple and hard.

returning

there will always be something missing,
trailing the dust, whisked away by the past.
there will be avenues unconquered,
places looked at, merely explored
and never known.

there will be things that i will go through
and not pause at or stop for,
doors i won't consider to push or to gently sway,
nerves and thoughts in my body
that i will never discover, never act out.

there will be men crowding Maqoma Street,
Centenary Hall, the Library Gardens,
chalk lines disappearing in dust –
and our grief as we arrive at these places,
realizing we have been led astray.

shadow

for Shepherd

he brings alone a shadow
in a dish full of night, full of
shallow stars –
no men bow down here, for no eternity
do we pray.

they ask you and ask God
the stone on which you lean, the flower
you bring –
the knees on which we heal.

finally, today this saturday

in the sea at night centimetres above sea-level
i have read cesar vallejo with a candle in my hand

finally, today this Saturday in October,
finally, at once, i know nothing about God and the blue sky.
of course they'll all say Mxolisi was right, after all –
they'll all say with their cerebral mothers
and their physicians and their dicotyledonous leaves –
they'll all say, ... and the hour would have darkened.

and the town Khiwo was striking 7
denouncement heavy on its sleeve. and 7 architects
from the reeking taverns, with clamour on the face
exhaustion of heat and heartache of the soul
delivered to me this disconsolate news –
"Murder of Mxolisi Nyezwa by hundred men!"

now it's easier to say
for all the chips are verily down, Netherlands where they all
came from is now a poor soulless country,
its statisticians have accounted for the 7 skeletons —
under the sea's algae, already dead in the algae
some men are praying for us.

and much more simply than us, here today, finally!
there's judgement for the clear skies, judgement for the dark
sorrowful nights
which is judgement for all men, the scaffolds
with names beginning with A
sculpted vertical across the index finger –
already on this side of the Richter scale
i can see my shoes, 2 shoes.

songs of rage and contentment

I

it is clear
this outline of the sea, this african in the land
this world in my soul
is the forbidden city, my native land.
this flower in the sun
like a painful sore is festering
it is what is sick, growing weak in the brain
in the place of suffering.
it is what is cold and dying, what i'm soon to know
and what every shooting star knows
and what every child knows.

in south africa, with my eyes closed
i write these words
i have a sense of new life
an ideal society
in the depths of the land.

it is what a plain blabbering man is muttering
— that you didn't hear,
what the roots and the bulbs in their soot will leave behind,
what i didn't wear with my pants
to match the broken string, what lies alone
above the warm petals
in the flowering of spring.

it is not what this or that witch is saying
not what we never heard in zimbabwe
with our eyes closed –
not what we didn't see against the scaffolds of time
dancing nakedly in the cold rain.

and i was afraid to say
i wanted so much to speak,
at the sign of 3 the torn trousers
were ripped off from my limbs, and what i had
remaining was a disease
at the terrible entry
at the root of the dusty town, what i had
was the sound of madness eating away
the aubergine
at the complications of the sick child.

this is the lounge, this is the horn of
the breaking teeth,
the brilliance of an african day.
and they wrapped the locks of reason
in the emptiness of distraught.
and the madness won't end at the terrible entry
of thieves –
seventy years, and our blood doesn't cease —
not inside our lungs
nor in our hearts of songs
nor in our songs of merriment
madness doesn't arise from the trees with their leaves,
nor in our bodies is the madness, nor in our limbs.

and the voice of distraught
its circuitous silence
like thunder
in seventeen years
keeps rolling

and the cold laments of the
rivermaids
the granite rocks
which walk
their seventy years

and the whisper of songs
of flowers
to a wind,
the joy of madness
in the morning
stream.

II

i have it in my paean, this magical oriental of spring
this outburst of flowers
the hysteria of spring –
the sparrows in the woods are laughing or dead,
a happy delirious fellow now
is every african!

a moonlight is springing in my eye, its water clear.
in my heart
like blazing guns
a happy peristalsis,
a rebellion of blood.

this evening my soul is delighted.
this evening
i am a happy-rested fellow
from the winter of your love,
the summer that scorches the body to black coal.

africans with hapless souls will die incessantly,
praying despicably
to the folks with three numbers,
the cross of wailings –

nothing comes of it, the wood of the dead fire.
nothing.
the dead body of the child in the black well.

III
sometimes i will talk
nobody listens
sometimes there's nothing in the air, no soul
near the hearth
no shadow in the balcony –
sometimes there's nothing to say to anyone
there's no food, no candle in the passages

> *what i didn't see*
> *couldn't uphold*
> *couldn't torment*
> *didn't find beautiful –*

sometimes there are no promenades
in the wind,
only a handful of blessings
in the dark valleys
in the miracles of my mind.

i'm holding my bones together, i'm caressing my skin
which is sad
which refuses to cry for me
so that every whisper in the house knows
so that everything i know is all i know:

my finger burning its skin
in several layers,
my foot that sets its path firmly on the soil
and with a schoolgirl's heart
i cast the pebbles of my secrets from my lips to steel.

i feel i'm the burnt child
who wakes alone without a body,
who sees the world with new eyes
and asks no questions.

> *what is born every moment*
> *is bludgeoning my skin*
> *what has fled everyday*
> *is blabbering its freedom.*

and the lonely child must know
where is the body to feed
where is the ethereal justice
where is the vine, the stalk to dry
where is the sound of the blueberry bird
the tune to sing to –

and the lonely child must know
where is the moment in unrecorded time
that passes history in its pages
to snatch the trembling leaves
to rob the flowers of wood.

IV
i believe in you earth, my brother, my friend
believe in you
in all my existence
(and the freedom of chaos shall reign in our land)
and i a fly that buzzes towards your shoulders, your fires
for hours
and hours on end.

i believe in you in light
and in darkness, in black sin
with all its sinful forces.
and i feel your springing torment
i feel your body like it was my ladder,
a law to be obeyed,
a gibbet!

i point to the womb in your womb.
and i need you to touch me
to embrace me like the sea,
to receive me in your arms
to tell me this world is good.
and the beat of unease is poisoning my mind,
and i stop alone, amongst the dying
at the appearance of silence.

i believe in you
like the flower in the flower.
i believe in you in matter and in decay
at the sad procession of death
at the beginning of living.
and there's an oddity so awesome
in all of this,
and i've been conscious of this foreign pain
as if it was mathematics.

i measure every word i say
like it was easy to be a poet.
and i wonder:
have all our joys landed
and have we begun to feel the cold?

V

in the dusty roads in the village of Zenani i met him.
his features gleamed, the entire frame of his skeleton white,
the extremity of his pointed nose extending extremely
towards the african sky.
he had a miser's double-chin, and he carried his
fat body like a King; he had the cruel whip
of the Master, his circumstantial inquisitive stare
and he carried a bayonet and chewed bubble-gum;
a smile like a cruel curse
feigned the outlines of the temple
and his evil blood coursed the veins
like the killer whale in the devious sea.

i slapped the black corruption of commerce
i blew the slave ships towards the hellish seas –

VI

A year is a timeless tree, a flower with no leaves. A year can be
brokered, you said. History is negotiable.

Here I know the screams of children. Day after day the diatomic
moles – history and words. Day after day I struggle to be myself,
to keep awake – to be a woman. I cringe what people fear. What
nobody knows.

In America you told me you have a name for everything – the benefits of an advanced country ruled by white people. Here you agree it's hard to be a woman. You can be faithful to yourself or to your country, but you will not know the land. In Africa there are no free antelopes.

I'm sitting here at the wayside inn, my hands swollen and aching deeply with pain. I fell on them when I climbed over the fences and the walls and the bushes – all over the place, as I ran away from you. From the anger of your friends. Both my knees are bruised. I've torn some ligaments. I cannot walk. I've got scars all over my face, and over my legs. My pants are torn.

conversations

1

i say constantly to God:
leprosy is everything in the bone
with its own sea and its own sadness;
and from the north pole its disease all comes down
in one go, bearing its cross
and wearing its guise –
dying as always in someone's palms.

2

it is good to be trivial when the time allows
for men like termites will gnaw and tear at your soul,
and in New Brighton at the strike of 10
simply hijack your soul.

3

sometimes all our lives sing out of tune,
all in a choir with a single purpose,
everything in many directions is spoken out,
aloud there.

4

sometimes we talk of trivial things,
of nothing at all.
and only there my brother
each piece of human sadness pierces the winter air like a bang,
throttles in its ribs
a gulp of air.

morning

i can see nothing to change my views about disaster —
how i wish i could see the turn of tides beginning,
the spider spinning the web, the blowing whale
and all the things in the sea.

i look at simple things which survive to bring life to all,
like many stars in bright rasp constellations,
my milky way breathes its fire there, my stars like fire
are blooming there.

and into my eyes the light in brilliant colours is beamed,
smoothed over, until in ruby colours it shines,
leaving they said a mere speckle
its gold and bronze transitions there.

no way

there's no way of feeling the dark size
that is empty or sad –
                    the bugger-up of everything.

there's no way
where the fire burns without token,
the mutiny of life rages on
like the fires of hell.

there's no way i know
under the rock
where the mildew weed blooms.
there's no way that is real where the cave opens
and where i hear the gone-out sound of breath,
the mother of all graves.

i will go and speak with the sea
to release its mysterious monster
from the carpet of its seed
where nothing matters
and where human forms lurk
constantly
adding to our woes.

there's no way amongst many suns
for the blue dust of death to perish
or to flow.
there's no way to vindicate my sin.
there's no way to open up my mouth
and cry.

talking again

i'm starting to talk without remorse
i'm starting to beg the beggar at the door
for sixty cents,
and my disasters wear long masks
with embroidery like earthlings
and i get up every day
with a pack of six or tea
every minute
the cry of human human in my howling ear.

and my pain is no less than the day before
Monday, and today i can't stand it!
the itching on my beard
with all its trimmings
grows with greater despair, bigger strides
like a colossus,
and i hurt much more
that my suffering is never done
that i'm melancholic
with a suffering that has no end.

woman

woman on earth
i feel your sun
i see alone your shadow against the moon's tail
the lyric, the tale
that falls slowly from
towards and between your hair
the whispers, the scandals in your name:
like a dove from above
i fall
alone –
towards you.

love

I

i'm in your shoulder, in the green blossom
of your thigh holding aloft the light
and our confirmations of love.

i reach the loud stars in the fire
where the blue butterflies fly and all spiders display the spinneret.
i leave a warm lamp in the corners where you last slept
quietly in the rain with nothing to wear.

in dreads i hear death remembered
in bitter years.
down the stairs i proceed in attics
where someone beckoned his last rustling
of breathing leaves.

and i will reach the heavens to touch the snow
that cuddles in your hands,
all the earth we left behind
in our forests of thirst and consuming snow.

II

it is plain
it is you and me, not the enormous snow.
it is life still in the tiny vein along the purple stream,
along everyone's back where the years clearly left
the erudition of cartels of men.

the hunch-backed man has his satans of dreams,
the gold-fish carousels the night's end.
the whispers and rattles of naked songs
bob-in and prod the iron fists
in my standing catastrophes of winds.

and he is nowhere with the sadness of joy
and the jagged melody of millions of men, there are others
clearly whispered inside the corridors of shame –
all the children that whispered our prayers,
every fish that danced its caches of joy.

and it is plain, it is our heart that touches
tenderly the melodies from the moon and from the stars.
the cold blood and the white milk that the heaven shades
in the penumbra of its stride. the silence and essence
of powerful souls parched together in perditions
and silence of dreams.

no longer

i have stopped making demands
upon the world.
i am smitten,
i have ridden a lame horse
like a matador in snow.

i have stopped looking around
and looking all over and about,
i have closed my eyes with tar,
bloated my consciousness
with ash.

i am no longer bereaved,
i have found myself

lilies

i breathe.
so are the symbolic gestures of thieves.

i'm thankful that i'm alive
i'm overwhelmed by the blackest chaos
(he is my protector)
and his eyes are black or blue
his hounds guard the morose sea.
and nothing's new
neither the voice as they say my name
neither my poetry.

my labour is a huge nettle of snow.
sorrow grows and reaches heaven,
where i can never be.

in the black earth
the figure of the Madonna makes its promises

in the black earth
we won over our conquerors

in the black earth
we sweat with our hands forever

i shall leave to where the gods send me
after my sentence
where they grow their lilies
and herbal leaves.

i won't forget

for Tate

even though it becomes hard,
i won't forget
to plant a flower in the night –
at night the sky is cold, the sea never settles,
at night i won't forget to remember
to put on the light, to forget to lead
the men out at sea, with a cold chill on their back,
gathering war with weakened hands.

i won't forget these men who tug at night
and who sleep in the bay
with hope of seeing light,
the blue light of the next day.

i won't forget how spring turns out and turns in
the sprig of summer
that lapses out, the frigid mystery that is gone –
strange people fill up the streets,
broken glass cuts through twines
keeping the child to its juvenile mother.

i won't forget that we are men on this earth
with numbed emotions,
nabbing at shadows
hidden from sight.

i won't forget how tough it is
to plant a flower in the wind,
to start a garden in the sand,
to raise a child in the ghetto.

i won't forget that man who walks alone at night,
who listens for God in every street,
whose dreams are like the ship's beacon,
in the stillness of each haunted night.